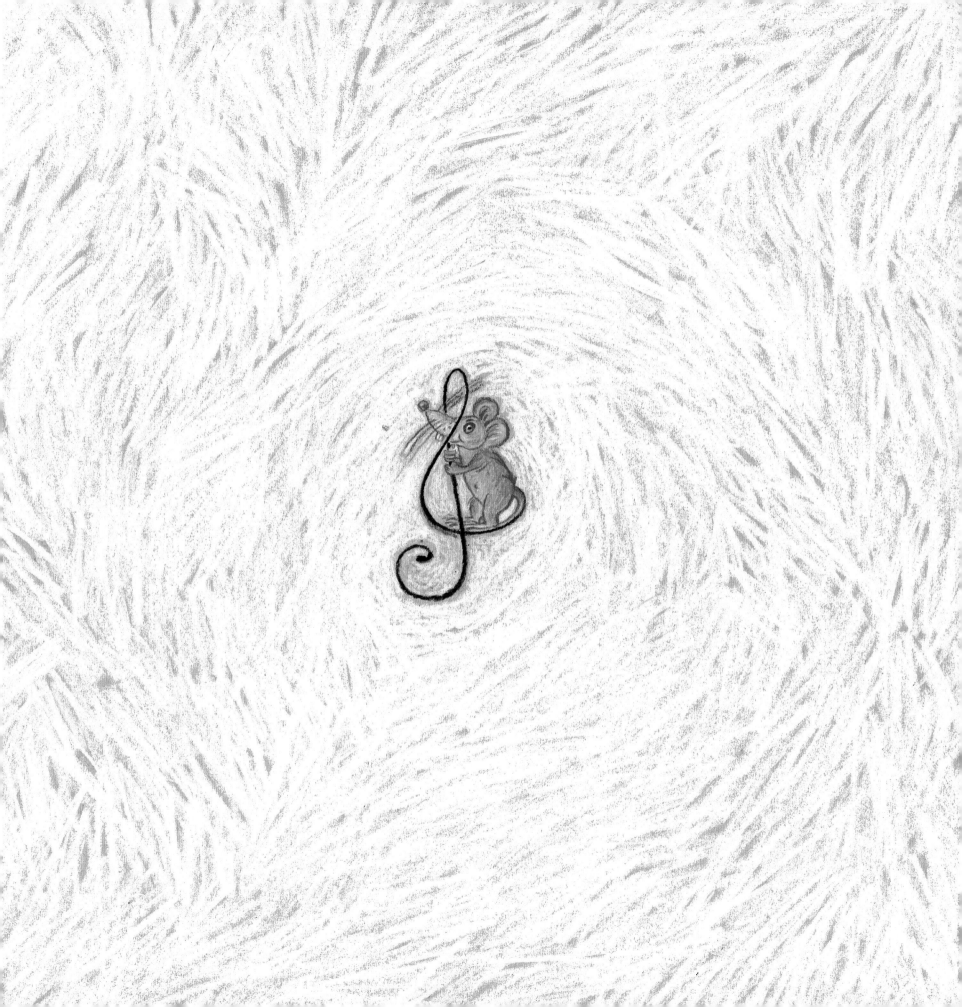

For those I love
T. C.

Pour Robin
M. F.

Text copyright © 1997 by T. C. Bartlett
Illustrations copyright © 1997 by Monique Felix
Jacket design by Rita Marshall

Creative Editions is an imprint of The Creative Company, 123 South Broad Street, Mankato, Minnesota 56001.

Library of Congress Cataloging-in-Publication Data
Bartlett, T. C.
Tuba lessons/by T. C. Bartlett; illustrated by Monique Felix.
p. cm.
"Creative Editions."
Summary: While walking through the woods on his way to his tuba lesson, a boy becomes sidetracked by all the animals that want to hear him play.
ISBN 0-15-201643-0
[1. Animals—Fiction. 2. Tuba—Fiction. 3. Stories without words.] I. Felix, Monique, ill. II. Title.
PZ7.B28433Tu 1997
[E]—dc21 96-44584

First edition

F E D C B A

Printed in Italy

TUBA

T. C. BARTLETT illustrated by MONIQUE FELIX

LESSONS

CREATIVE EDITIONS mankato HARCOURT BRACE & COMPANY san diego new york london

"Now, don't dillydally in the woods, young man, or you'll be late for your tuba lesson!"

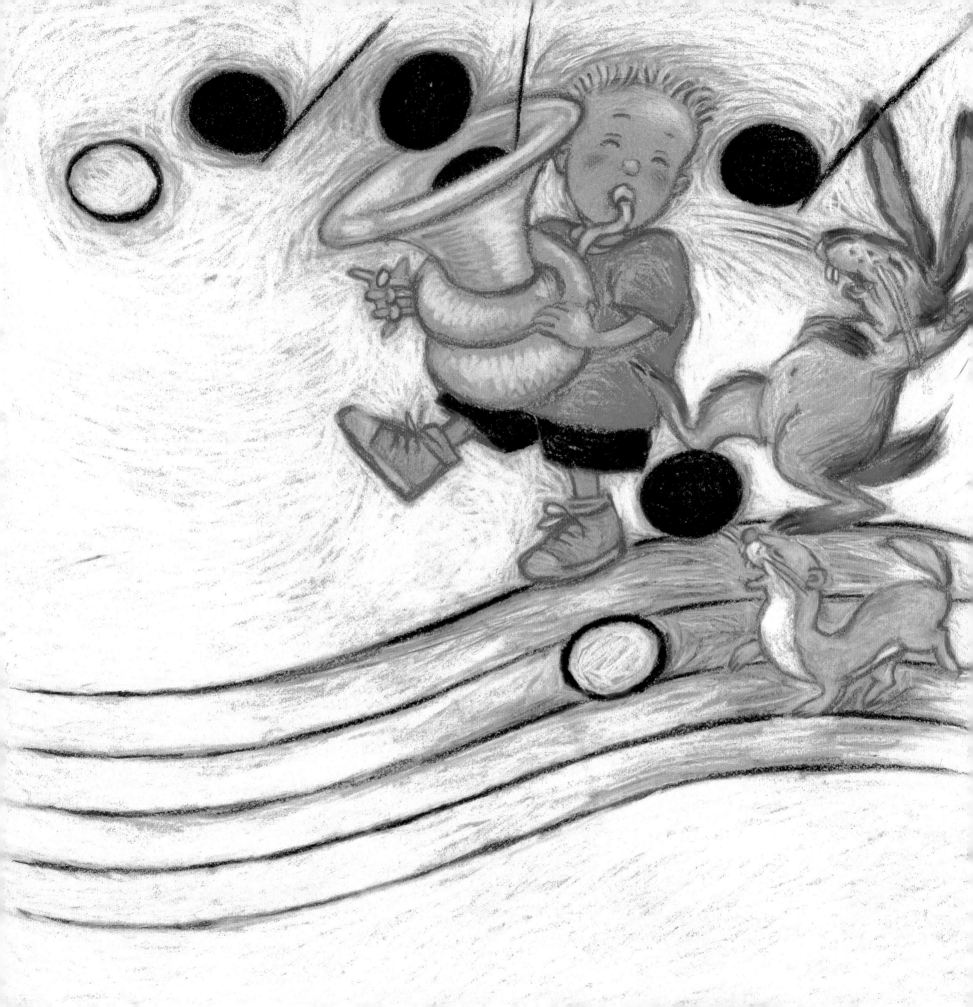

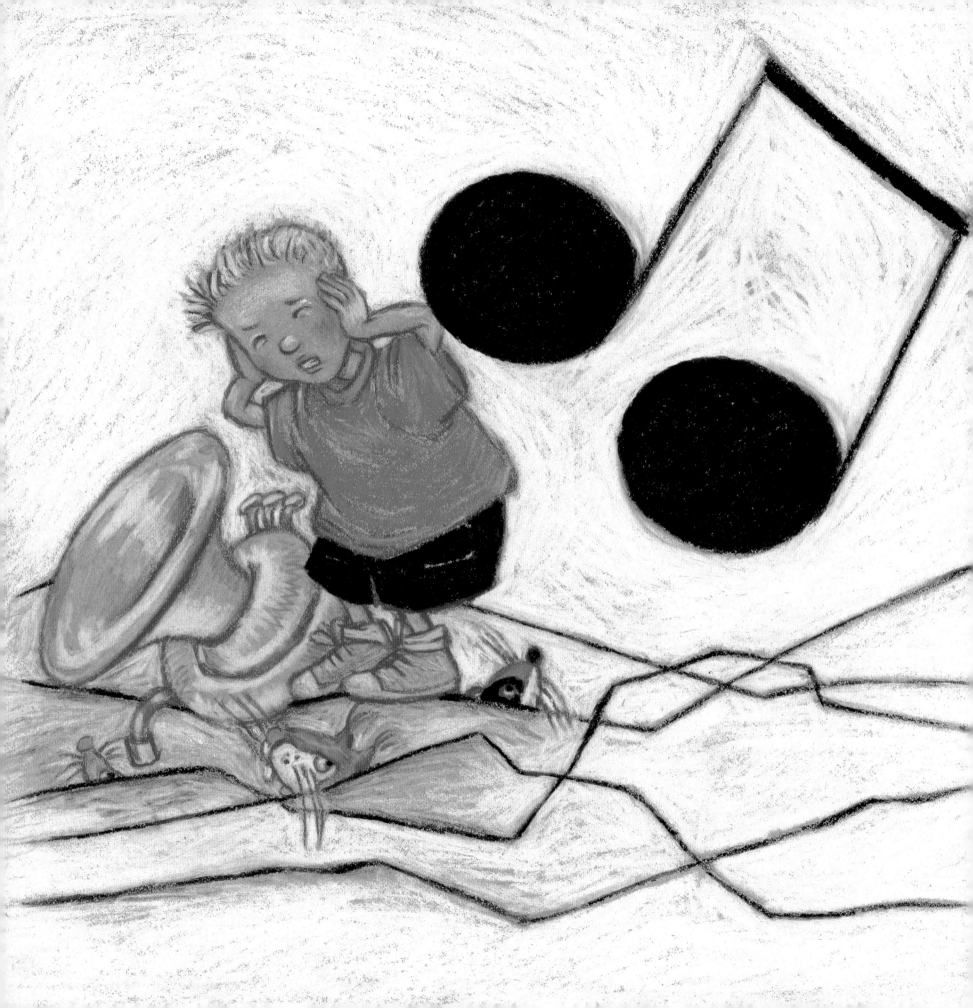

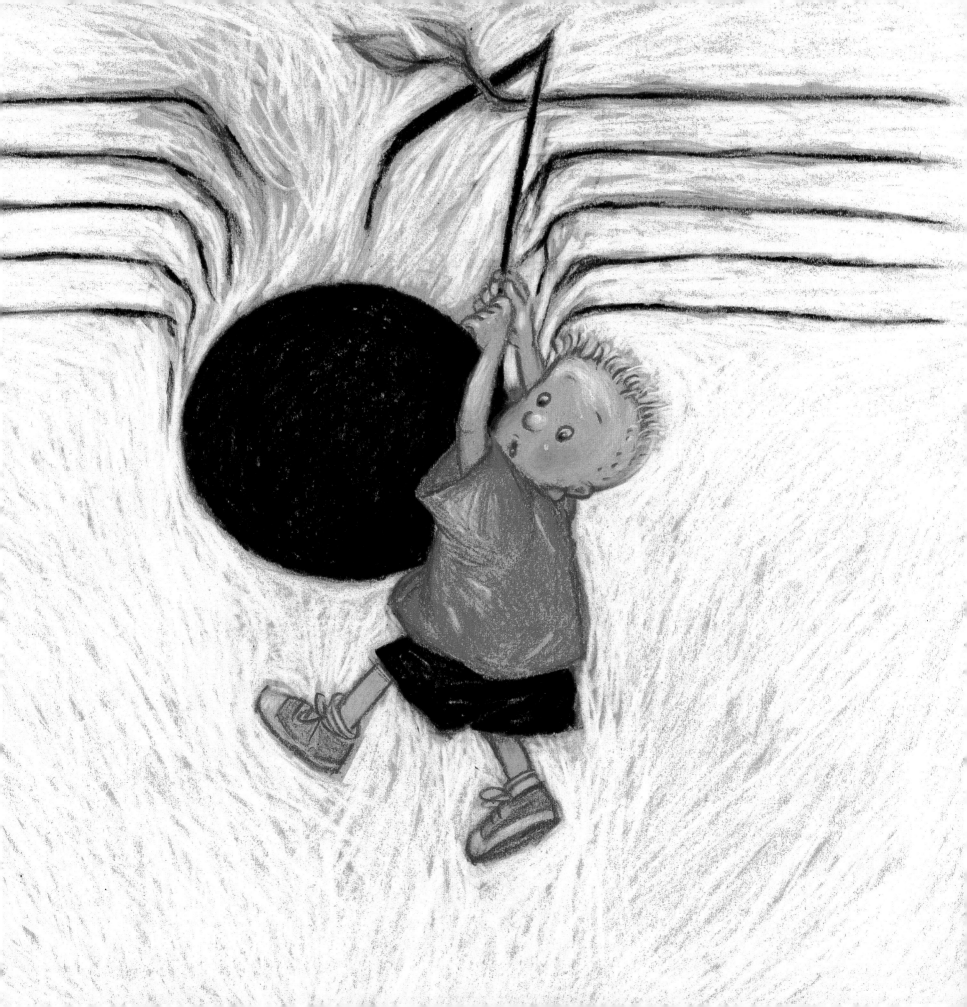

"Young man, you're late for your tuba lesson! Next time you'll get an extra hour of practice!"
TUBA LESSONS

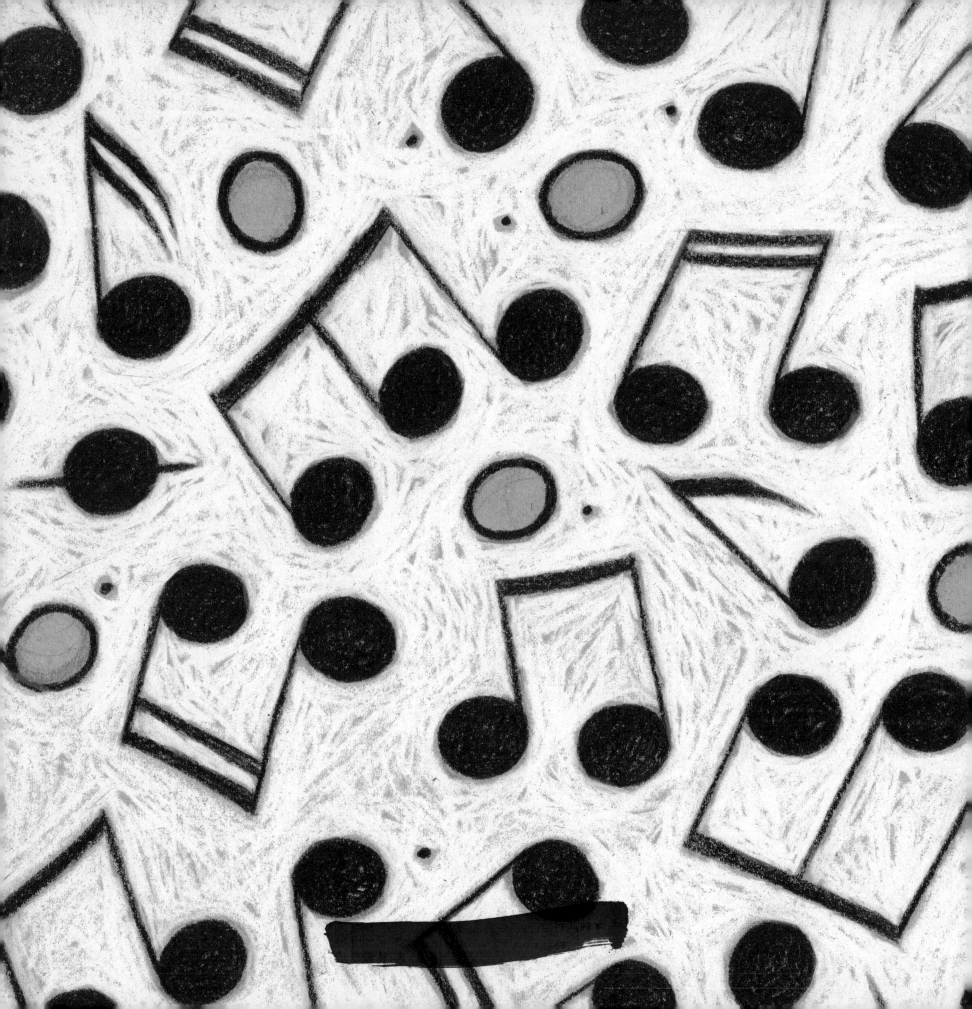